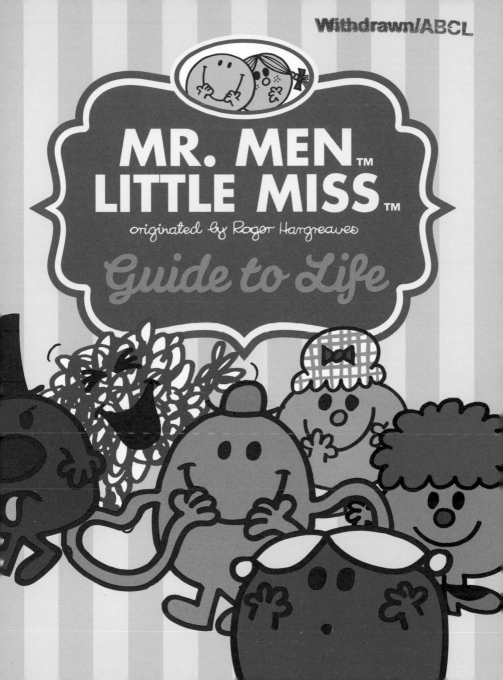

MR. MEN™
LITTLE MISS™

originated by Roger Hargreaves

Guide to Life

PRICE STERN SLOAN
Published by the Penguin Group
Penguin Group (USA) LLC, 375 Hudson Street, New York, New York 10014, USA

USA | Canada | UK | Ireland | Australia | New Zealand | India | South Africa | China

penguin.com
A Penguin Random House Company

MR. MEN **LITTLE MISS**
by Roger Hargreaves

Sanrio®

USED UNDER LICENSE SANRIO, INC.
Sanrio
USA

SIL-5018

www.mrmenlittlemiss.net

Photo credits: pages 6, 10, 20, 26, 32, 36, 42, 48, 49, 55, 62,
63: (postcard) © AnnaSivak/iStock/Thinkstock; page 29, 30, 31:
(playing cards) © Christos Georghiou/Hemera/Thinkstock.

Published by Price Stern Sloan, a division of Penguin Young Readers Group,
345 Hudson Street, New York, New York 10014. *PSS!* is a registered
trademark of Penguin Group (USA) LLC. Manufactured in China.

ISBN 978-0-8431-8108-1   10 9 8 7 6 5 4 3 2 1

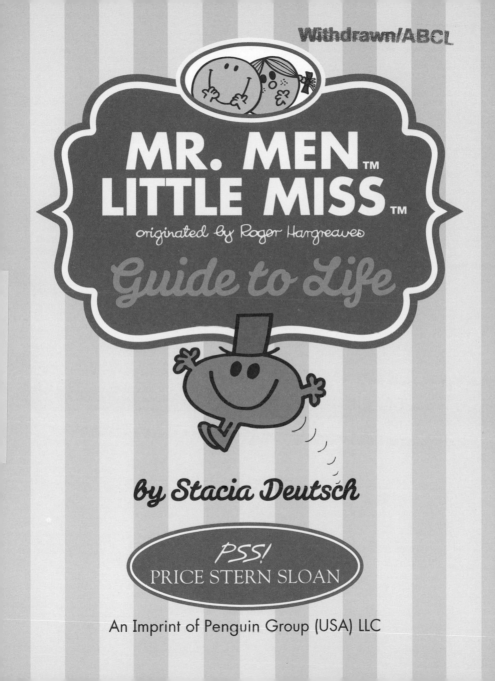

MR. MEN™
LITTLE MISS™

originated by Roger Hargreaves

Guide to Life

by Stacia Deutsch

PSS!
PRICE STERN SLOAN

An Imprint of Penguin Group (USA) LLC

Table of Contents

Dear Mr. Lazy,

What are the best plans for a relaxing weekend?

Sleepy Schlump

Mr. Lazy

Dear Sleepy Schlump,

It's smart of you to ask me. You caught me just at the right time—between naps. If you lived in Yawn Cottage in Sleepyland, you'd already know the answer to this one. Sleep in! Don't get up until the afternoon. Like exercise, this may take some practice. Resist the urge to get out of bed.

Once it's officially afternoon, you can get up, but only when you're so hungry that you couldn't possibly stay in bed another minute. That's how you know it's time for breakfast (which is really lunch). While the tea is boiling and the toast is toasting, you can catch a few extra zzzz's.

After you eat, you'll be tired from being up so long, so it's the perfect time for a long nap. **Sleep till dinnertime**, eat quickly, and run back to bed.

Oh, yawn. I'm getting tired.

YAWN

YAWN

Since you're planning a relaxing weekend, you can sleep straight through to the next day and do it all again!

Things to remember to make a lazy weekend even more perfectly lazy:

—If your friends call, don't answer the phone.

—No checking e-mail or texts

—Do not answer the door.

And most important, DO NOT LET

MR. BUSY OR MR. BUSTLE RUIN YOUR REST!

Time for me to go. I need a nap.

Exhausted,

Mr. Lazy

ZZZZZzz

Dear Sleepy Schlump,

Little Miss Busy here. Don't listen to Mr. Lazy. No one can sleep all day! Well, no one except Mr. Lazy.

Get up. Tidy up. Sweep the floor. Dust. Scrub. Polish. Plan a vacation. Read a book. Learn a language. Then do it all again!

Call your friends and answer the door when they ring the bell. Don't be like Mr. Rude. Manners are important. You should even make your friends some lunch. Ask them to stay. Play a game, ride bikes, have a barbeque, go for a swim, walk the dog . . .

Oh my.

I have to go.

So much to do.

Take my advice, and you will have a fun and fabulous weekend.

Good-bye for now,

Little Miss Busy

PS: You should consider changing your name to something more active. Always Awake, perhaps?

Mr. Rude

Little Miss Busy

8

Mr. Uppity's Amazing Tips for Becoming Rich (and Miserable)

Mr. Uppity

1. **Collect coins.** Change from the store. Foreign money from traveling. Pennies you find in the couch.
2. Find a container to put them in.
3. Fill your container to the top.
4. Then get another container and start again.
5. Here's the most important part: Don't spend your collected coins. Do not share them with your friends.
6. **Better yet, don't have any friends.** Sit in your house and count your coins. If anyone tries to speak to you, be rude. Never say "Please" or "Thank you."

Do as I say and you'll be rich and miserable in no time flat!

Dear Little Miss Scatterbrain,
How do I stop
forgetting everything?!
From Someone Somewhere

Dear Someone Somewhere,

I understand your problem. It's hard being someone from somewhere. I wish I knew where I lived, too.

Maybe you should ask someone around you where you live. I wonder if it's Buttercup Cottage.

Remembering is very hard. There are some tricks I learned to help me when I need to remember really important things. I hope my tricks will help you.

I wrote them down so I wouldn't forget. And to make sure I didn't forget where I put my list of how to remember, I stuck the list under my hat.

Now, where did I put my hat?
Maybe Mr. Forgetful can help us.

Sincerely,
Little Miss Scatterbrain

Dear Some . . . body,
What was the question?
From Mr. . . . .
Oh dear, I've forgotten.

New Message

To: mrhappy@happyland.com
From: frowningfrump@misery.com
Sorry to bother you

Dear Mr. Happy,

I hope you don't mind me e-mailing you. I have a question for you: How do I get to be as happy as you?

Appreciatively,

Frowning Frump

New Message

To: frowningfrump@misery.com
From: mrhappy@happyland.com
Re: Sorry to bother you

Dearest Frowning Frump,

You're being no bother at all! Do you live anywhere near Happyland? Happyland is truly the happiest place on earth, so you should plan a trip here someday. You could stay at my cottage by the lake, at the foot of a mountain, in the woods.

While you plan your trip to visit me, let me give you my best advice.

Little Miss Brainy once told me that science has proven that there are three things everyone should do to be happier.

1. Take care of your body. Eat right, exercise, and get enough sleep. Simple as that!

Little Miss Brainy

2. Help others. For example, walk Mr. Lazy across the street (he'll be grateful for the exercise, and you'll be happier than before you did it), have an extra tissue handy for Mr. Sneeze, or help Mr. Clumsy with a clean-up project. I'm sure he has a few!

3. Smile. Mr. Miserable discovered how important smiling is when he came to Happyland with me. Try it. It really does take more muscles to frown than it does to smile.

Best to you,
Mr. Happy

New Message

To: mrhappy@happyland.com
From: frowningfrump@misery.com
Re: Sorry to bother you

Thank you for your response. But what if it doesn't work? What if I can't be happier? What if I fail?

New Message

To: littlemissbrainy@happyland.com
From: mrhappy@happyland.com
FW: Sorry to bother you

Hi, Little Miss Brainy—See Frowning Frump's e-mail. I'm running out of ideas. Could you kindly respond?

To: frowningfrump@misery.com
From: littlemissbrainy@happyland.com
Re: FW: Sorry to bother you

Dear Frowning Frump,

It's Little Miss Brainy here. Mr. Happy forwarded your e-mail to me. Don't worry. No one can be happy all the time, not even Mr. Happy. So give yourself a break. Focus on the good things that happen instead of the bad ones. Go outside and look at the flowers, birds, and trees. Feel the sunshine on your face. Relax, and have fun!

Yours truly,

Little Miss Brainy

PS: If you have any harder questions, send them right away. I'll be glad to answer them. The harder the better.

Little Miss Naughty's Instructions for the Perfect Prank

What you need:

—Plastic cups
—A pitcher of water
—A place to do the prank

(A hallway is an excellent choice.)

Little Miss Naughty

Fill each cup about halfway with water and set it down on the floor along the back wall. Then put another row of cups with water in front of that row, and so on. Put the cups close together, so no one can walk between them. Back out of the room or hallway, setting out row after row of water cups, wall to wall in tight lines. Keep going until the entire floor is covered. Make sure there are cups with water over the whole space. You can put them on tables, chairs, windowsills . . . HA! The more the better.

This prank takes a while to set up. But it'll be worth it when you see the eyes of your parents, friends, or teachers who know they can't get to where they need to be without spilling water!

Now just wait for someone to come by.

Hee-hee!

LMN

(When pulling off a prank, never sign your real name.)

Mr. Nosey

Dear Prankster—
Don't do it! Don't listen to Little Miss Naughty or you'll get your nose tweaked! Ask her. She'll tell you I am right. No prank, no matter how funny, is worth a red nose. **Trust me on this one.**

—Mr. (Sore) Nosey

Mr. Nosey

Prankster—
It's still worth it. Noses heal. Laughs are forever.
LMN

Mr. Strong's Tips on How to Get Strong

Here's a secret you might not know: You don't need to own weights to get stronger. You can do push-ups in your bedroom, no special equipment required.

Put your hands flat on the floor with your palms down. Focus on tightening your stomach muscles to keep your body straight. Lift your body up like a bridge, then lower yourself to the ground. Keep your eyes facing forward so you don't bend your neck. Keep going. Slowly, slowly. When you hit the floor, push yourself up—that's why it's called a "push-up." Easy, right?

Mr. Strong

If you really want to be strong like me, do push-ups every day, all day long. All your free time should be spent doing push-ups.

And don't forget to look in a mirror and flex. Wear short sleeves so everyone can see your muscles, too. Everyone will want to know how they can be like you. Soon they all will be doing push-ups, getting stronger, and feeling happier—thanks to you!

Dear Mr. Snow,

Why can't it be winter all year round?

Frosty Friend

MR. MEN LITTLE MISS
GUIDE TO LIFE

Dear Frosty Friend,

Mr. Snow

What an excellent question! You *can* have winter all year round. All you need is your imagination and your very own snow globe.

I'll teach you how to make a snow globe. Then when it's warm outside, just shake the globe and—ta-da! A chilly winter dream is yours any day you want.

You'll need:

—A clean glass jar with a tight lid

—Plastic animals, rocks, laminated pictures, etc.

—Glue

—Cold water

—Glitter

—Glycerin (optional)

—Electrical tape

1. On the inside of the jar's lid, create your scene. Glue plastic animals, rocks, or laminated pictures of yourself securely. Make sure you keep things away from the edges of the lid so it will still fit on the jar. Let it dry overnight.

2. Fill the jar with water. Use cold water—freezing, even. It works better. Let the water reach almost to the top, but not all the way. You need room for your decorations.

3. Stir glitter into the water. Add more glitter than you think you might want, since it'll settle at the bottom. You can add a dash of glycerin (from a craft store) to the water to keep the glitter from clumping into "snowballs." But personally, I love snowballs. Oh, this is so exciting. We're almost done.

4. Carefully put the lid on the jar and seal it tight. Wrap electrical tape around the seal so it doesn't leak. That's part one . . .

Yours,

Mr. Snow

Hi Frosty,

Mr. Snow asked me, Mr. Daydream, to take it from here. He said I'd be better at explaining this part, since I am an imagination professional.

So your snow globe is all ready. Here comes part two of the explanation for how you can have winter all the time.

What you need:

—Winter clothes

—A quiet place to sit and hang out

—Your snow globe

First, get dressed for winter. Don't forget your gloves, scarf, and hat. Next, find a nice place to sit, where no one is going to interrupt you or wonder why you are wearing a parka in the summer. Get comfortable.

Now, shake your snow globe. Stare at the falling flakes. Imagine yourself

Mr. Daydream

running and playing in the lightly falling snow.

Shake it again. This time imagine yourself sledding down a big hill. There's no one there but you, so go as fast as you want. It's totally safe. Shout "Wheeee!"

Shake the snow globe one more time. Imagine that you have built a snow fortress and stocked it with snowballs. Mr. Snow guards the entrance. You are ready to face any summer-loving invaders—and here they come . . .

Snowball fight!!!
You win. Obviously.

When the battle for the fort is over, it's time for a snack.

Take off your snow clothes. Shake the snow off your feet. Blow warm air on your hands. Then go to the kitchen for a cup of hot cocoa.

Have a fabulous winter all year round.

Cool dreams,

Mr. Daydream

To: wondering@ilovepets.com
From: littlemisshelpful@happyland.com
Re: Should I adopt a cat or a dog?

Dear Wondering,

Well, first I need to know: are you a cat person or a dog person? Do you like rambunctious walks outside no matter the season, or do you prefer quiet cuddles and cat-and-mouse games at home?

If you prefer the former, you're a dog person, so get a dog! I'll come over to help. I'll play with your new friend and take it for walks. I can teach it tricks like "sit" and "stay," and how to fetch a ball.

I promise I won't lose your dog at the park. I won't let him run in puddles. Or jump fences. Or eat leaves. I won't let him dig a hole that other people might fall into. Or get his head stuck in a bucket.

And most importantly, I promise your new dog won't end up in a lake.

Please get a dog. Please?

Unless, of course, you prefer quiet cuddles and cat-and-mouse games, which means you're a cat person, and you should get a cat. But I'll still come over to help!

I can teach your cat tricks like "chase" and "pounce." I promise I won't let your cat scratch up the furniture. I won't get it wet. **I won't let it escape from the yard.** I definitely won't let your cat get stuck in a tree so high we have to call the fire department.

Nope. I won't do any of those things.

Please get a cat. Please?

Actually, dog or cat, whichever you choose . . . you can count on me! **I want to help!**

Sincerely,

Little Miss Helpful

Dear Mr. Sneeze,
How can I stop
sneezing?
Achoo Achoo

MR. MEN LITTLE MISS
GUIDE TO LIFE

Dear Achoo Achoo,
Don't try to stop. Sneezing is very healthy.
When you sneeze, you're protecting the body from
harmful germs that could cause sickness. Something
bad tries to sneak inside your nose, so—ACHOO—
your body tosses it out again.

It's quite amazing how it all works.
Sneezes are very interesting. Did you
know that no one can keep their eyes open while
sneezing? And that sneezes travel about one hundred
miles per hour? Once we
had a race: Little Miss Quick
versus a sneeze. The
sneeze won!

Some people think that your
eyeballs can pop out when you

Little Miss Quick

sneeze or that your heart stops. Other people think you can predict the weather with sneezes. I don't think any of these things are true, so don't be like Mr. Worry. It won't hurt you to keep on sneezing.

Now, Achoo, the question is: How long have you been sneezing? The longest recorded sneezing bout was 978 days. I should have beaten that record, but Coldland isn't cold anymore. I just don't sneeze like I used to in the good ol' days.

If you are close to 979 days, I say, "Keep on sneezing!" Don't stop now.

Achoo to you,
Mr. Sneeze

Mr. Sneeze

PS: If you really are serious about not sneezing and you have a cold, here are some tips for getting healthy: Drink lots of orange juice; have some hot water with lemon and honey; eat kiwis and chicken soup; and most important, get lots of rest. If you have allergies . . . I guess you'll just have to wait them out!

Little Miss Magic's Favorite Magic Trick

All you need is a deck of cards and a friend. It's best to pick someone who thinks they're really smart, like Mr. Clever or Little Miss Brainy, to do this trick on. They'll spell the name of each card and that card will magically be the next one to appear!

A bit of advice: Do not invite Mr. Tickle to your magic show. His devious gangly arms get in the way of magic. I say this from experience.

Before your smart friends arrive,

Little Miss Brainy

Mr. Clever

Mr. Tickle

set up your deck of cards. Take out all the cards in one suit and put all the other cards aside. I like hearts. Arrange the cards in the following order:

Five (on the bottom), Nine, Ten, King, Jack, Two, Four, Six, Queen, Ace, Seven, Eight, Three (on the top).

Now, open the door and let your genius friends in. Be sure to offer them a snack and a drink, not because of the magic trick, but because it's nice.

Then, hold the deck over the snack table. You will spell the names of the cards in order: A-C-E—move one card from the bottom to the top of the stack as you say each letter. Then after the

Little Miss Magic

"E," flip the next card from the bottom of the deck. It will be the ACE. Place that card on the table.

Then do it again, spelling out loud, "T-W-O" and moving them from the bottom to the top of the deck again as you say each letter. The card right after the O card will be flipped. Ta-da! It's the TWO! Put that card faceup on the table on top of the ACE . . . and keep on going. Spell out THREE, then FOUR, FIVE, SIX . . . through JACK. As you go, flip the card after your spelling is complete. It's like magic.

When you get to Q-U-E-E-N, you will only have two cards. After N you will flip over the next card and amaze your friends that it's the QUEEN.

The last card in your hand will be the KING.

Show your friends the KING and say, "Voila!" Then, take a bow.

The next day, invite over different friends. A good trick should be repeated. Good snacks should be repeated, too. Have fun!

Dear Little Miss Late,
How can I walk into my classroom after class has already started without anyone noticing?

Sneaky Shoes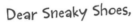

Dear Sneaky Shoes,

I find that it's better not to try to go anywhere on time. Don't make plans—that way, you're never late! But . . . on those rare occasions when you do need to go out and meet someone, or when you have a job, or when you must go to school, there's only one thing to do.

Tiptoe.

If your shoes make noise, take them off and walk in your socks. When you get close to the place where you are supposed to be, drop down onto your hands and knees and crawl through the door. Hold the handle while the door closes behind you so it doesn't bang.

When you get inside, rise up to put your hands on your knees and inch forward. Pretend you're invisible. If anyone looks at you, don't look back. They might blow your cover.

With tiny steps, move to the nearest empty seat. Slip into the chair, being careful not to bang your knees on the desk. If you do bump the desk, don't yell "Ow." Just sit up straight and smile as if you've been there all along.

Happy sneaking around,

Little Miss Late

Little Miss Late

Mr. Grumpy's Guide to Frowning

A good frown requires eleven muscles, and most importantly, the right attitude. So first, think about something you're upset about. Then think about something you're more upset about. Now think about something even worse. You've got it!

To start off, make your eyes crinkle. Then wrinkle your chin and pull down the corners of your mouth. Then close your mouth and wrinkle your brow. Good job! You're using the eleven muscles needed to frown.

For a deeper frown, you can use more muscles.

My personal goal is to use more than eleven and to keep that frown going all day long. There are approximately forty-three muscles in your face. You might as well engage them all for the perfect repellent expression.

Mr. Grumpy

Little Miss Giggles's Guide to Laughing

Laughing is the best way to deal with anything in life. Take it from me—grinning, giggling, and chuckling will definitely make you happier than frowning, grumping, and complaining. And I guarantee it'll brighten other people's days, too!

Here's how to do it: Tug on the corners of your mouth to broaden it. Then raise the corners of your mouth. Bring your smile to the sides of your face, tug on the corners of your nose and mouth, and crease the corners of your eyes. Great job—you're using the twelve muscles needed to laugh! Now think about something funny and chuckle away.

Make sure to use these muscles all day long. Maybe even work in a few more for an even heartier laugh. And remember, laughing is contagious!

Little Miss Giggles

Dear Little Miss Lucky,

What kind of lucky charm works the best?

Accidents Abound

Dear Accidents Abound,

Is that truly your name? You always have accidents?

Oh dear.

Well, then, you're going to need a lot of lucky charms.

All lucky charms work equally well. For you, though, I'd suggest getting as many charms as you can carry.

Start with a four-leaf clover, a cricket, a ladybug, and an acorn. Then, you should get a horseshoe,

Little Miss Lucky

some pennies, and a dolphin. For even more luck, you're going to need a pot of gold, a rainbow, and a wishing well.

Don't forget to feed the dolphin.

If you can't get any of those things, then you should do what I do: Stay home. Snuggle under the covers. Read a book. Go to sleep. That way, you'll have lucky dreams, like me.

Sincerely,
Little Miss Lucky

To: <u>mrnervous@happyland.com</u>
From: <u>scaredstiff@boo.com</u>

Does Bigfoot exist?

Dear Mr. Nervous,

The subject of this e-mail says it all. Please answer my question as soon as you can!

Gratefully,
Scared Stiff

To: <u>scaredstiff@boo.com</u>
From: <u>mrnervous@happyland.com</u>
Re: Does Bigfoot exist?

Dear Scared Stiff,

Of course Bigfoot exists. And aliens. And the Loch Ness Monster. The only way to be entirely safe is to stay at home. Lock your doors. Close your shades. That's my best advice.

There are documented stories from America and Asia over the past three

hundred years about people who have seen Bigfoot, also called Sasquatch. It's not just one Bigfoot, either. They live in groups. You have to be very careful when you go outside. Check over your shoulder a lot and watch where you walk. You don't want to run into a Bigfoot by accident, and you definitely don't want to make a Bigfoot mad.

I can tell you because I saw one once. It was a long time ago, but I can remember it as if it were yesterday. I was in the woods at night, wandering around by myself. The Bigfoot I saw was huge and hairy and walked on two feet. You know Bigfoot chases away people by roaring and throwing rocks, right? If I close my eyes, I can still hear that ferocious roar. My head still hurts where that rock hit me. I can show you where my bruise used to be.

When I get very nervous, I like to count to ten and take deep breaths to calm myself down.

In the case of Bigfoot, I'd suggest if you see one, don't take pictures and don't start counting. Run! I'd even suggest you buy some new sneakers, just in case.

Stay safe,

Mr. Nervous

Mr. Nervous

To: scaredstiff@boo.com
From: mrbrave@happyland.com
Re: Fwd: Does Bigfoot exist?

Dear Scared Stiff,

Mr. Brave here. Mr. Nervous sent me your e-mail, and I decided to respond to you. Don't listen to Mr. Nervous. Most Bigfoot sightings are fake. Scientists who study what people think is Sasquatch poop usually discover that it's deer poop. Videos and photographs almost always turn out to be other animals or tricks of the light. People often see bears and think they saw Bigfoot. Sometimes people make up Bigfoot videos to get famous.

So far, no one has caught a Bigfoot, and no one can prove without a doubt that one exists. Not even Mr. Nervous.

There's only one way to be sure that Bigfoot exists.

If you're still suspicious, Scared Stiff, let's do an experiment. Grab a sleeping bag and a flashlight. Bring your camera. Let's find out for ourselves if there really is a Sasquatch.

Meet you in the woods at midnight,
Mr. Brave

Mr. Brave

PS: Bring those sneakers, just in case.

CONTEST

How Many Things Can You Name That Come in Pairs?

Winning Entry from Little Miss Twins:
Socks, shoes, boots, weekends, arms, legs, feet, hands, front teeth, chopsticks, earrings, dice, gloves, dumbbells, ice skates, skis, snowshoes, headlights, knitting needles, windshield wipers, wings, lungs, eyes, shoelaces, slippers, kidneys, ears, lips, crutches, slippers, wheels, you and us!

Congratulations, Little Miss Twins!

Dear Little Miss Scary,

How can I frighten
my neighbors?

Horror Haunt

Oooh, Horror Haunt,

If you shout "Boo!" really loud, your friends
and neighbors will run away screaming. I know.
I'm the best scarer there is! Ask anyone who
lives near Scary Cottage. (Although, I must
admit, Mr. Nervous and Mr. Noisy can be pretty
frightening when they want to be . . .)

If shouting "Boo" isn't enough for you and
you want to make your scary scares even scarier—
you need to add drama. And the way to do that
is . . . fake blood!!!!

Fake blood is amazing. You can use it to dress
like a zombie, a werewolf, a vampire, or someone
who is bleeding from a gushing wound.

So get ready for some extra-terrifying,
freakishly gruesome frights. Do not save this

for Halloween. The best scares are when no one expects them!

You'll need:

—1 tablespoon water

—3 tablespoons golden corn syrup

—A few drops of food coloring (red and blue and green)

—A spoonful (or more, as needed) of cornstarch

Yikes. I'm shivering already.

Little Miss Scary

1. In a bowl, mix the water with the corn syrup. Add a few drops of red food coloring and stir. This will be bright red. To make more realistic blood, put in a couple drops of green and blue, until it's a lovely dark maroon color.

Exciting, right?

2. Now put in some cornstarch to thicken it. Add a little at a time and stir until it's the perfect thickness. If little clumps form at the top, you can scoop them out.

3. Dip your finger in the mix. Is it the right color? Does the tip of your finger look like you cut it off with a meat slicer? If not, you can add more food coloring to get the perfect look. A zombie needs darker blood than a vampire because its blood is old and decayed. I'm an expert on zombies and vampires, so if you want to know more, just ask!

4. Let the mixture sit for ten minutes so that it thickens. Waiting is hard, but I promise it'll be worth it. Use the time to plan your costume. Make a list of the people you are going to scare.

5. Before you know it, it'll be time. Decorate your face, your arms, and your body . . . then put on your darkest clothes. Be careful because the fake blood will stain your clothes.

Tiptoe outside.

And . . .

"BOOOO!"

Happy Haunting,
Little Miss Scary

Little Miss Birthday's Guide to Giving the Perfect Birthday Present

1. Think about your friend or family member. What does she or he like to do? Is there a joke you like to laugh about together? Music you both enjoy? Something they would love but would never get for themselves?

2. Now, dig a little deeper. Is there somewhere you visited together? Is there something special you did together? The thinking part is the most important thing . . . you'll find yourself smiling at all the great memories. That's the gift's gift to you!

Little Miss Birthday

45

3. Don't tell anyone what you're thinking about. No hints. The surprise is part of what makes gift giving so much fun.

4. Now it's time to go shopping or make the gift. The great part about this step is that if you're shopping, it won't take long, since you already know what you're getting! If you're making something, getting the supplies won't take long, either, because you already know what you're making!

5. Now that you have your gift, wrap it. A nice-looking present beats something thrown in a brown bag any day.

Happy Birthday

6. Next, make a card and write something meaningful on it. Cards are the best part.

7. Give your gift and card! Gifts for birthdays are wonderful. And the most wonderful thing is that every single day, there's someone who has a birthday!

Mr. Birthday

Dear Mr. Good,
When should I write
a thank-you note?
Grateful Guest

Dear Grateful,

Thank you for asking for advice about writing a thank-you note. It's good to be grateful. In fact, you should always thank everyone, for everything. If someone catches your hat, or carries your groceries, or opens the door for you, you should thank them.

Saying "Thank you" is good. Writing a thank-you note is even better!

You should hurry and immediately write a note if someone gave you an especially thoughtful present for your birthday or wrote a wonderfully meaningful answer to your letter.

I look forward to hearing from you soon.

Best wishes,

Mr. Good

Mr. Good

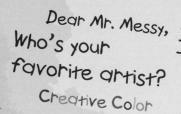

Dear Mr. Messy,
Who's your
favorite artist?
Creative Color

MR. MEN LITTLE MISS
GUIDE TO LIFE

Dear Creative Color,

YOU will be my favorite artist if you make crayon art. I'll teach you how. I'm warning you . . . it's messy!

You need:

—A box of crayons

—Glue

—A hair dryer

GLUE

Mr. Messy

1. You're going to need to use all your crayons. Remove all the wrappers. Glue every single crayon to the living room wall. That's right— just glue them straight onto the wall. Never

mind the wallpaper or paint. After this, you'll never have to hang a picture again. Your family will love you for it.

2. If you want to make messy art but think **Little Miss Neat and Little Miss Tidy** might not be pleased, you can glue the crayons to a piece of cardboard or a canvas from the art store. Put paper on the floor under your project. Staying clean ruins the fun, but this way you might not get grounded for the rest of your life.

3. Next, check that Little Miss Neat and Little Miss Tidy are NOT around. If they are, send them outside to do the gardening. They like that.

Little Miss Tidy

4. Now, use the hair dryer to melt the crayons. They will drip down toward the floor like little wax rivers. If you're going for maximum messiness, let them run all over the floor.

5. When Little Miss Neat and Little Miss Tidy come inside, don't let them clean up. Don't let them give you a bath. Put your hands on your hips and tell them that you like being messy. Just like me.

6. Now, let's go mess up the bedroom. Then the kitchen, the bathroom . . . Oh, there is so much to do.

Mr. Messy

To: <u>littlemissstar@happyland.com</u>
From: <u>starstruck@ilovecelebrities.com</u>
From your biggest fan!!

Dear Little Miss Star,

I'm a **HUGE** fan of yours. I hope you don't mind my contacting you via e-mail! I was wondering if I could get your advice.

How do I meet someone famous?

Many thanks in advance.

Lovingly yours,
Starstruck

To: <u>starstruck@ilovecelebrities.com</u>
From: <u>littlemissstar@happyland.com</u>
Re: From your biggest fan!!

Dear Starstruck,

I don't often respond to my fan e-mails, but I decided that yours warranted an answer. The best way to find a star is to go to the places stars hang out. I hear there's a city in

Southern California that's really popular and an island that belongs to New York State. Are those close to you? Any big city might work, but you'll have an easier time if you go where there's a large concentration of stars. Don't wait for them to come to you. That might not work very well.

So now that you are in a place where there are celebrities, you need to find out where they hang out. Let's pretend you want to meet me.

You could come to my home at Twinkle Cottage, but most celebrities don't just answer the door and let strangers in. It's better to find them in public.

For example, you could try to find me at a book signing. Look in the newspaper, and you'll find places I am scheduled to visit. Maybe you'll discover that I'll be at a new restaurant opening.

Little Miss Star

Or at a concert. Movie opening nights and awards shows would be other places you might find me.

Then plan what you're going to say to me. No point in meeting your heroine and saying, "Blah blah blattity blah blah," right? I see it all the time, so make sure you don't make this mistake. Practice if you want to take a photo or ask for an autograph. Personally, I love to be in pictures. I have a wonderful smile, if I do say so myself.

If I *am* giving you an autograph, ask me to personalize it by telling me your name. You'll enjoy it more, and it will be proof to others that you met me.

The most important thing to do when you meet me is to be nice and be yourself.

Come find me at my next book signing. I'll save you a place in line.

Forever Famous,
Little Miss Star

Dear Mr. Impossible,
How can I do impossible things, like you?

Doggedly Discouraged

Mr. Small

Little Miss Tiny

Dear Doggedly Discouraged,

Nothing's impossible. You can jump over a house, walk up a tree, or stand on your head with no hands if you really put your mind to it. Just tell yourself, "It's possible."

I had a friend who thought his math problem couldn't be solved. He'd also never read a book upside down. I showed him how to do both.

So now, what can you do?

Mr. Impossible

Anything you want!
You just have to try.

If you want to jump over a house, start with a small house. If you want to be invisible, begin in a place where you're alone. You'll need to flap your arms if you want to fly.

Now, I am going to tell you a secret that I have never told anyone else: Trying is just the beginning. You need to practice to get really good at the impossible. And at the end of every day, grin your impossible grin and then fall asleep standing on your head.

It's all possible!

Sincerely,

Mr. Impossible

Mr. Perfect's Instructions for How to Be Perfect

Have you ever heard the saying "Practice makes perfect"? I feel like Mr. Impossible might have told you this already. Well, it does. You just need a little practice.

At my birthday at Tiptop Cottage, it took all my perfectly perfect skills to make the party perfect. I welcomed my guests politely. Danced delicately. Cleaned up without complaining. Made cakes. And said "Thank you" for every gift.

You, too, can have a perfect day. Here's the plan. Follow it perfectly precisely.

Mr. Perfect

1. Wake up early, giving yourself plenty of time to get ready. Brush your teeth, wash your hands and face, get dressed, make your bed, and put your dirty clothes in the hamper.

2. Have a healthy breakfast. Wash your dishes and put the milk back in the refrigerator.

3. Put everything you need for the day in a bag. Check the time so that you aren't late to school. Brush your hair and smile at yourself in the mirror.

4. Make your own lunch. That way you know you'll like it.

5. Put on your shoes and leave home with time to spare.

6.   Work hard at school. Do your best. Pay attention in class. Respect your teachers. Raise your hand when you have a question. Treat your friends nicely. Oh, have fun, too.

7.   After school, when you get home, do your homework right away. I call it "Have to's before want to's." That means to finish what you must do before you watch TV or play video games and hang out.

8.   Eat all your vegetables at dinner.

9.   While you are having a meal together, share the most interesting things from your day with your family. Go around and take turns. Be a good listener to others.

10. Clear your plate after you are finished eating. Offer to help wash the dishes or take out the trash. No grumbling. Being tidy is part of being perfect.

11. Shower, change for bed, and read a book.

12. Set your alarm and get to sleep early so that you'll be rested and ready to do it all again tomorrow.

Mr. Busy

Enjoy this schedule. I think it will work just right for you. Just follow it exactly as I wrote it, and you will find that all your days will be as wonderfully perfect as mine.

Best,
Mr. Perfect

This sounds terrible. We protest!
There's no need to be perfect.
Signed,

Mr. Grumpy

Little Miss Naughty

Mr. Lazy

Little Miss Trouble

Little Miss Bad

Mr. Uppity

Little Miss Stubborn

Mr. Grumble

Mr. Worry

Little Miss Contrary

Mr. Slow

Mr. Rude

Mr. Messy

Dear Little
Miss Somersault,
How can I set a
world record?
Rolling Ragged

Dear Rolling Ragged,
I think you could beat the world record for somersaults. All you have to do is a mere 8,342 somersaults. No problem. I usually do that before breakfast.

So get into position and roll. If you get dizzy . . . just don't stop. Throwing up is fine, but stopping isn't. So go, go, go.

I can't wait to see your name in the record book!

By the way, here's the deal: I'll let you have the title for a month, so enjoy the fame!

Flippingly Yours,
Little Miss Somersault

Little Miss Somersault

Little Miss Sunshine,
How can I brighten someone's day?
Best Buddy

Dear Best Buddy,

You've already brightened my day, simply by asking!

I made a sign for the King of Miseryland, and he really liked it. In fact, the sign made him smile. You can make a sign for your buddy, too, but I have an even better idea:

Just open your arms wide and give someone a hug.

I promise that a hug will lead to a smile. A smile leads to a laugh, which leads to a chuckle, which leads to a giggle . . . Which means that no one will be sad anymore—not ever again!

So get out there and start hugging. You should start brightening someone's day right away.

I'm counting on you to spread smiles!

I'm sending sun-shining days to you now and always,
Little Miss Sunshine

Little Miss Sunshine

Good-bye from all the Mr. Men and Little Misses! And remember to keep asking questions!